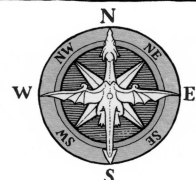

The DRAGON *Ark*

WRITTEN BY

Curatoria Draconis

EDITED BY

Emma Roberts

ILLUSTRATED BY

Tomislav Tomić

MAGIC CAT 🐱 PUBLISHING

NEW YORK

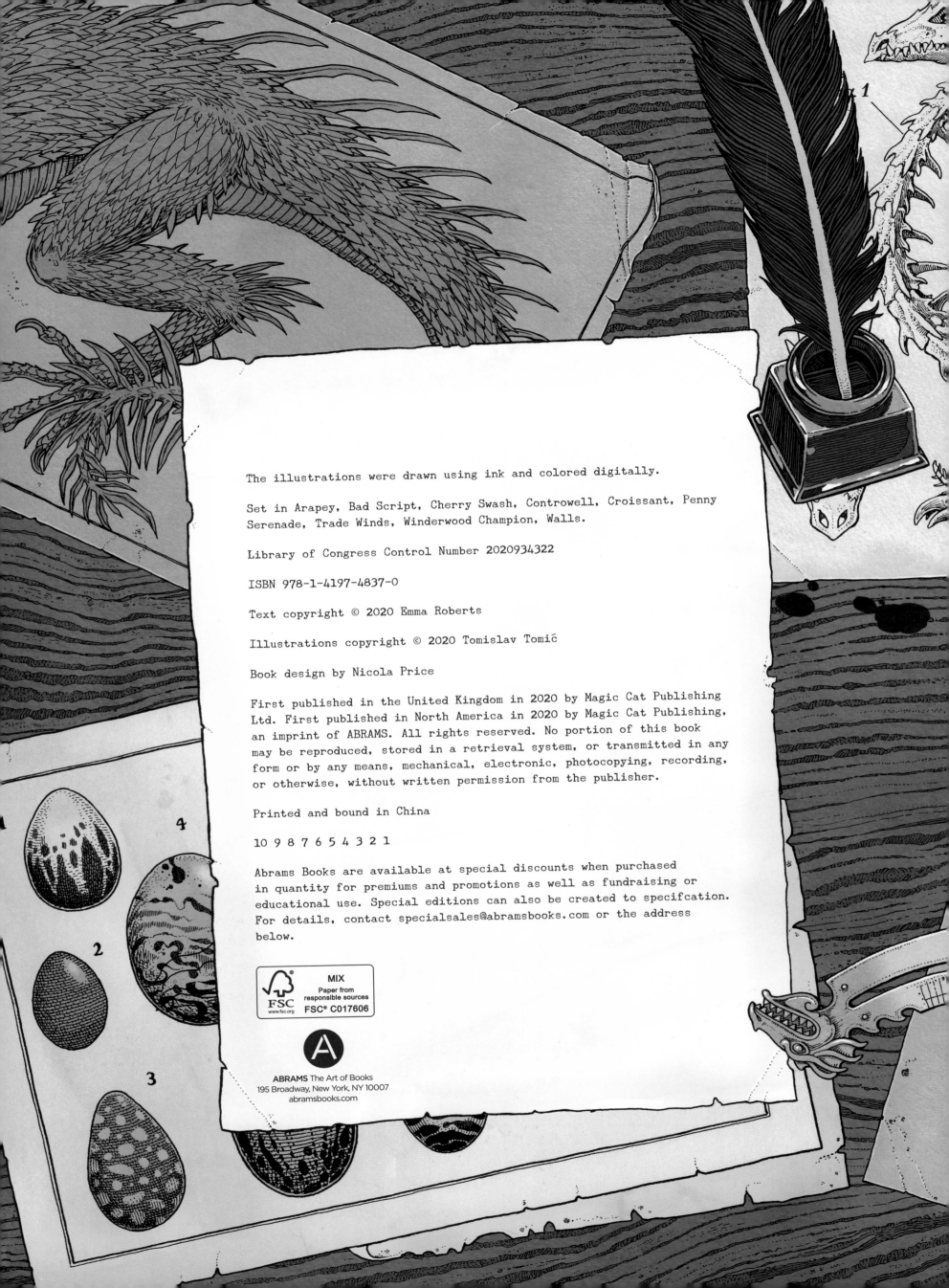

The illustrations were drawn using ink and colored digitally.

Set in Arapey, Bad Script, Cherry Swash, Controwell, Croissant, Penny Serenade, Trade Winds, Winderwood Champion, Walls.

Library of Congress Control Number 2020934322

ISBN 978-1-4197-4837-0

Text copyright © 2020 Emma Roberts

Illustrations copyright © 2020 Tomislav Tomić

Book design by Nicola Price

Printed and bound in China

10 9 8 7 6 5 4 3 2 1

Abrams Books are available at special discounts when purchased in quantity for premiums and promotions as well as fundraising or educational use. Special editions can also be created to specifcation. For details, contact specialsales@abramsbooks.com or the address below.

MIX
Paper from
responsible sources
FSC® C017606
www.fsc.org

ABRAMS The Art of Books
195 Broadway, New York, NY 10007
abramsbooks.com

GREETINGS, FEARLESS ADVENTURER,

I am the Dragon Protector, the latest in a long line of a SECRET ORGANIZATION
of people who are sworn allies of all dragons.

The work of the Dragon Protector has become a matter of LIFE AND DEATH, as dragons find
their habitats and hiding places plundered and destroyed for natural resources.

The Dragon Ark is a vessel of protection and discovery; it offers refuge and help to all
DRAGONS. Some choose to live in our comfortable dragon stables and travel with us, others
we monitor in their natural habitats, bringing data back to the ark to aid our research and
understanding of dragonkind.

We know the whereabouts of EVERY KNOWN SPECIES of dragon on EVERY CONTINENT of the
globe. Except for one. The exquisite CELESTIAL DRAGON. The search for the celestial dragon has been
ongoing for centuries, but time is running out. We cannot risk the unthinkable—we must find it before this, the
most mystical of all dragons, becomes EXTINCT.

Are you ready to step aboard the Dragon Ark and embark on the
VOYAGE OF YOUR LIFE?

YOURS IN FIRE AND ICE,

CURATORIA DRACONIS

THE DRAGON PROTECTOR

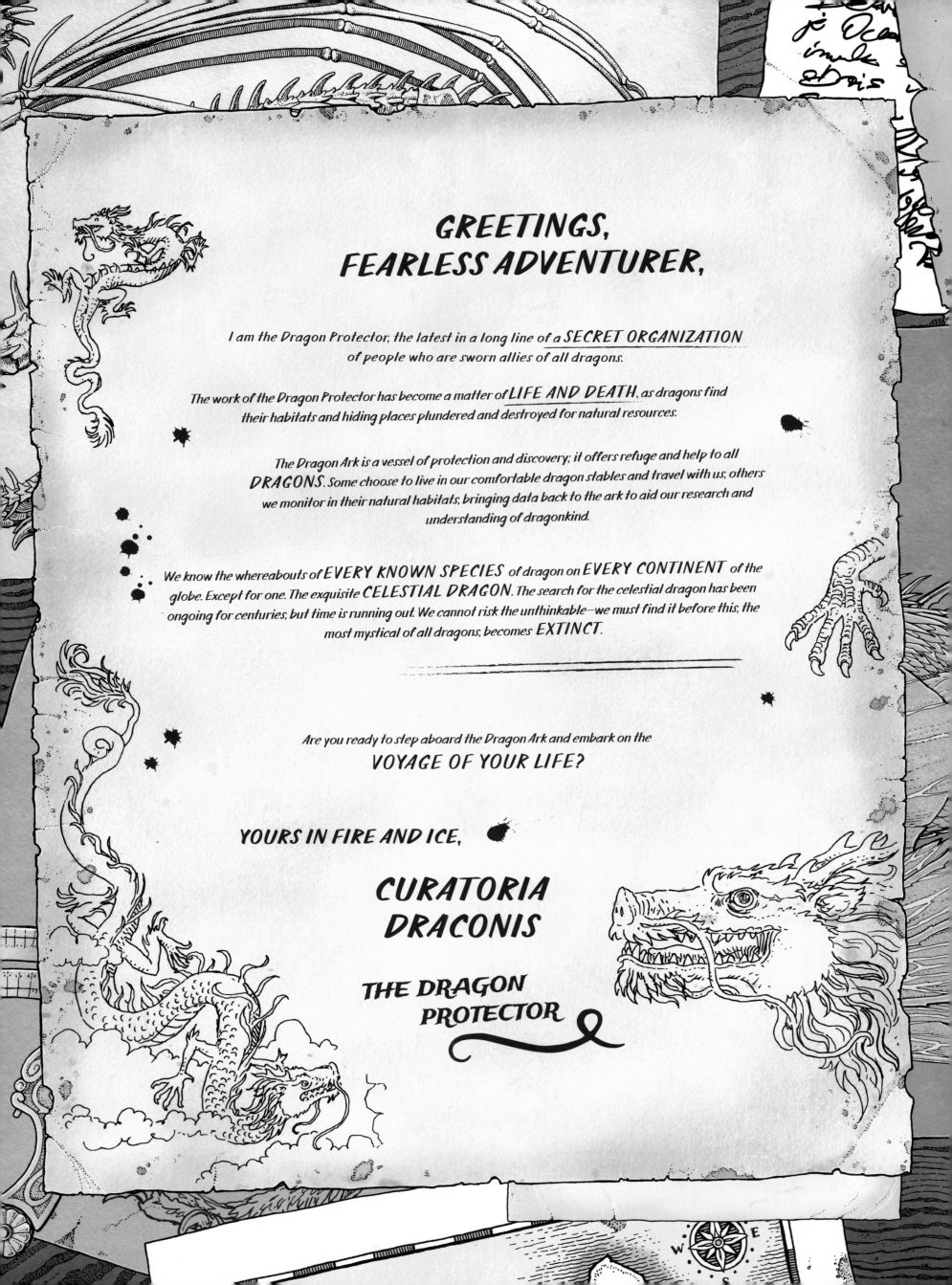

Crew Gallery

❖

The Dragon Protector personally chooses every member of their crew. Each is an expert in their field and can be relied upon for their fierce discretion. And, more vital perhaps, they all have one goal: to protect our precious dragons and their habitats. These are just some of the hard-working crew members aboard the *Dragon Ark*.

Curatoria Draconis

THE DRAGON PROTECTOR

Professor P. Howie

CHIEF HISTORIAN

Dr. Yiling Chen
MARINE BIOLOGIST

Dr. Jabu Kolisi
CHIEF MEDIC

Captain Aurelius
McGregor
CHIEF AERONAUT

Athena Mehta
LIBRARIAN

Nikolai Jacobsen
POLAR EXPLORER

Dr. Lexie Sun
RESEARCHER

The *Dragon Ark*

✦

Behold the mightiest vessel most people will *never* see. The *Dragon Ark* is a marvel of engineering and shipbuilding, designed by the very first Dragon Protector and adapted by each that followed to suit their needs. Our own Curatoria Draconis has expanded the upper deck exercise facilities available to the dragons and improved the catering in the ark's mess—for which the crew is most grateful!

Dining room

Crew's cabin

Antarctica quarters

Europe quarters

Africa quarters

Feeding prep area

Oceania quarters

The Dragon Protector's Quarters

Welcome to the Dragon Protector's private space—not only a place she comes to read, research, and relax, but also a place of safekeeping for the treasures entrusted to the Dragon Protector by dragons all across the earth. Each Dragon Protector decorates their quarters to their own taste, and we all agree that this is one of the most stylish yet.

OCEANIA

TERRAIN FOCUS

lofty peaks
and lush canopies

The realms of Oceania offer dragons a terrain that is rich and varied. For some, the hot, scorched plains are perfect territory for learning to breathe fire undetected. Others love lofty peaks such as Aoraki/Mount Cook, which provide instant cloud cover for safe exercise and flight.

The depths of the ocean trenches in this part of the world provide the perfect place for sea serpents to find both camouflage and peace, although it sometimes proves a challenge for the Dragon Protector to locate and observe her dragons in the dark, mysterious waters.

Common Species of Dragon in Oceania

Our Chief Historian, Professor Howie, has voyaged widely in Oceania over many decades, gathering dragonlore from the dragons living there. One of the finest examples from the region is the limbless wurm.

Elongated nostrils
allow for faster release of noxious fumes

Wide belly scales
grip the ground, aiding in a concertina-like movement

Long, nimble tail
wraps and holds an enemy, even at a distance

WARNING

Approach with caution, dear apprentice! My team and I must always take extreme care when a wurm is on board the Dragon Ark. They do not have a pleasant nature, but there is always a place for them when they choose to come aboard. You'll notice we have deliberately created a dank, swampy environment on this part of the Oceania quarters. This is to mimic a wurm's preferred natural surroundings.

These dragons have a particular dislike of humans—built up over centuries of mistreatment. Should you approach a wurm, always make sure you do so with the protection of a gas mask and breathing apparatus. Wurms are known to emit toxic fumes purely for the pleasure of seeing their victims endure a slow, painful death. Please do try not to let this happen—I'm starting to become fond of you.

The Henbury "Meteorite"

Popular science tells us that the enormous craters at the Henbury Meteorites Conservation Reserve of central Australia were the result of a meteorite hitting the earth around 5,000 years ago. It is a closely guarded secret among the dragon community that the craters were actually the result of an overenthusiastic aerial chase between two colossal juvenile dragons that got a little out of hand.

Aerial chases can often appear more violent than they actually are. These young dragons are really just play-fighting in the skies.

The Wurm: a Brief Study

A wurm's fangs may be long and terrifying to behold, but in this dragon's case, its fumes are worse than its bite. With nostrils that are oversized to aid the emission of poison, it prefers to breathe out a deadly gas rather than tear a victim limb from limb.

Like tadpoles, which lose their tails, juvenile wurms shed their wings when they reach maturity, thanks to a particular enzyme found in their connective tissue.

It is thought that powdered wurm horn will make the recipient immune to all disease. No matter the foolhardiness of trying to slay a wurm in order to remove its horn, this barbaric practice is one the Dragon Protector seeks to eradicate.

In the dustiest section of my library, I discovered ancient field notes describing the pressures on Rapa Nui's dragons due to human overcrowding. How times have changed.

Rapa Nui (Easter Island)

The enormous stone statues on Rapa Nui have a fearsome guardian indeed. Living in the island's system of lava caves is a dragon who, according to other dragons of Oceania, pledged to protect the megalithic monuments centuries ago. Since many of the statues have been removed from the island by visiting explorers, this dragon has developed a reputation for sleeping on the job.

Sea Serpents in the Mariana Trench

In the most mysterious depths of the ocean, many miles below the surface, the determined dragon lover will find dragons of the sea serpent variety. This is the Mariana Trench, the deepest place in all of the world's oceans and home to a pair of taniwha dragons.

Deep-sea Dragons

Dr. Xiling Chen, the *Dragon Ark*'s marine biologist and submersible pilot, has returned from the Mariana Trench after a successful observation mission. Dr. Chen has agreed to share her notes from the field with you.

Taniwha, Mariana Trench

Remarkable sights from the submersible today . . . We are deep below the surface of the sea, with no sunlight at all, yet these cunning dragons can use their own light to lure curious prey! Bioluminescent bacteria in their snout generate light beneath a patch of transparent skin. We know that taniwha enjoy the thrill of the hunt, and when we dimmed our own lights we witnessed the male displaying this behavior, letting his terrified prey swim away before giving chase.

(Check with the Dragon Protector regarding bioluminescence in subterranean cave-dwelling species. Is it unique to deep-sea dragons???)

While observing the taniwha dragons, I noticed that these dragons are partial to basking in the jets of hot water spewed out by hydrothermal vents on the ocean floor. With the water at temperatures of around 725°F, these sea serpents display behavior similar to that of their volcanic cousins. My hypothesis remains that their scales have properties that enable them to resist both the freezing temperatures of the ocean waters at this depth and the direct jets of extreme heat. In most species, scales can usually resist one or the other, but never both with equal success. A sample of shed taniwha scales, found on the seabed, will be brought back to the lab for further testing

GUAM

fig.1

fig.2

We have been extremely fortunate to observe these taniwha in their true form. They are contrary creatures at the best of times, and sometimes choose to appear to humans as whales or sharks. In order to be sure that these dragons are healthy and not under threat, it is vital to study them in dragon form. When the time comes for you to return to these waters without me, you must always chant an appeasing refrain as you descend, to alert these dragons to your approach. They know the Dragon Protector means them no harm. Whether or not they choose to be observed will be another matter entirely…

The biggest danger in the oceans is not these colossal beasts, but the deadly scourge of plastic pollution. This threat to the world's seas has deeply affected dragons, none more so than the sea serpents, who risk swallowing plastic every time they feed. Sea serpents are deeply intelligent beings but cannot always prevent themselves scooping up waste plastic in their enormous jaws. Young apprentice, it will be you and your fellow protectors of nature who can defend the oceans, and dragonkind will thank you for it!

Now, we must set sail. Don't forget to hang your wetsuit to dry. They start to smell if you don't take care of them, and the dragons will complain…

THE DRAGON PROTECTOR

P.S.—In between dodging its poisonous fumes, I extracted a clue about the whereabouts of the celestial dragon from our not-so-friendly wurm.

THE CELESTIAL DRAGON MAY ONLY BE FOUND WHEN IN THE FIFTH ZODIAC YEAR.

We must try to collect more clues as we journey on.

NIWHA

THE NEW ZEALAND POST
HAS TUHIRANGI COME AGAIN?

Long said to be the guardian of the treacherous waters of Te Moana-a-Raukawa (Cook Strait), the taniwha Tuhirangi is believed to have appeared again, although this time not in its sea monster form of legend. Since 1888, a white dolphin has met and guided every vessel making its way through the notoriously narrow, rocky Te Aumiti (French Pass).

This fearsome taniwha is said to have been the guide for generations of voyagers over many hundreds of years, ensuring each and every one a safe passage.

Whether a sea monster in disguise, or just a kindly creature, this guardian dolphin has seen to it that not a single shipwreck has happened on its watch. Long may it stay in our seas!

C

ANTARCTICA

dragons in danger

The dragons who make their home in Antarctica are some of the hardiest in all of dragonkind. The icy terrain is extraordinarily beautiful, yet unforgiving, and dragons have adapted in remarkable ways.

With no indigenous population and no major settlements, the Antarctic dragons are able to live tranquil lives relatively free from human interruption. However, the accelerated thinning of the ice sheet that covers 98 percent of the continent is a grave and pressing concern for all on board the *Dragon Ark*.

Common Species of Dragon in Antarctica

Welcome to the chilly Antarctica quarters, where temperatures of 14°F mimic the resident ice dragon's natural habitat.

Ice horns as sharp as shards of glass are used for defense

Blue eyes are purely decorative, but terrifying up close

My dear apprentice, I do hope you are wearing your thermal underwear. I know many of us are averse to the cold, but I cannot stress enough how important it is for the Antarctica quarters to remain below freezing temperatures at all times. If ice dragons are exposed to temperatures higher than those they are used to in their natural habitat, they will melt. Not only would this make a dreadful mess, it would break the solemn vow I made as Dragon Protector.

Our laboratory has been studying the properties of ice dragon blood, but we must be vigilant with the security of our findings. A lab technician disappeared with important data not long ago, and I fear he has taken it to scientists working in the fledgling human science of cryogenic freezing. If it was revealed that the blood of ice dragons holds the key to successfully freezing and preserving human bodies after death, it could be more devastating to the ice dragon population than the melting ice in Antarctica.

Extra-long claw offers greater stability on icy ground, and particularly for takeoff

Dragons Teeth Rocks

A small group of black tooth-shaped rocks rising to around 320 feet tall lie off the coast of Astrolabe Island in Antarctica. Little do people know that these rocks mark the burial site of the very first ice dragon, who, after reaching an ancient age, died while out flying. The dragon fell from the sky and its body settled on the sea, where the rocks sprouted from its teeth.

Humans like to name natural phenomena after dragons, and none more so than those found in Antarctica. It is always with enormous pride that I remind the crew that we on the Dragon Ark are lucky enough to know the true stories.

The Ice Dragon: a Brief Study

Given the conditions in which they live, ice dragons are, unsurprisingly, rare. Food sources are limited in Antarctica. Beyond penguins, there's very little to satisfy a hungry dragon. However, fully grown males have been known to pluck blue whales from the ocean to feast on.

Much about an ice dragon will be familiar to those who study dragonkind— the serpentine body, translucent wings, and four powerful limbs. However, there are quirks that make the ice dragon family entirely unique—one example being its breath, which is not fiery but instead lets out a fierce blast of air at a subzero temperature, causing the blood of its prey to freeze immediately.

The ice dragon is able to camouflage itself easily in its habitat since its scales are pure white. Even its blood resembles melted ice and runs clear; enough oxygen dissolves directly into the fluid of an ice dragon's blood to eliminate the need for the protein hemoglobin, which among other things, is responsible for giving human blood its red color.

This dragon has graciously accepted the Dragon Protector's invitation to come aboard the ark so that she may study its blood in greater detail.

"Dragon-skin" Ice

The rare phenomenon known as dragon-skin ice draws scientists from far and wide. Their theory involves ice freezing in scalelike patterns due to very strong winds, but the reality is much simpler—a colossal, colossally lazy ice dragon has been asleep beneath the surface of the ice for some decades now. Whenever powerful winds blow, the real scales on the dragon's back are revealed.

Flight Training in the Beardmore Glacier

✦

Measuring 125 miles long and 25 miles wide, and with few human
visitors, the Beardmore Glacier is the perfect place for an ice
dragon to come and go as it pleases. The Dragon Protector has
witnessed this particular dragon's first steps as a hatchling and
now, its first clumsy attempts at flight.

The Dragon in the Glacier

✦

Journeying through a glacier is a very dangerous undertaking. The Dragon Protector is fortunate to have many experts in their field on board the *Dragon Ark*, and none more so than the famous polar explorer and environmentalist, Nikolai Jacobsen.

FIELD NOTES
Queen Maud Camp, 7:30 p.m.

I had the honor of leading the Dragon Protector in an Antarctic expedition when she heard rumors of a dragon egg discovered at the foot of the Queen Maud Mountains at the west side of the Beardmore Glacier. Returning to check on the young dragon today, we came upon the creature's first attempts at flight. It may have been clumsy, but still—I have never seen anything more majestic in all my years of polar exploration.

It was interesting to observe how the ice dragon's claws have adapted to the terrain, evolving into a formation not unlike the crampons humans wear for a secure grip when walking on ice. Multiple claws are arranged in a specific pattern around the foot, with one large claw at the front allowing the dragon to pivot on the ice while still sustaining its hold on the slippery surface. Although the young dragon is still mastering the basics of flight, it is clear that this claw formation makes for a faster run up and thus a smoother takeoff into the air.

As the Antarctic ice continues to melt as a result of climate change, I fear the Dragon Ark will soon see a large influx of ice dragons seeking refuge. It is a dire situation we find ourselves in and in the interest of dragons, as well as all living creatures, we must make our voices heard.

Frost Dragon

Not to be confused with the ice dragon, its bigger cousin, a frost dragon is migratory, seeking out the cold, and can be found in multiple continents. Flying in packs in the dead of night, these miniature dragons breathe out a delicate, frosty dusting which settles to create the icy patterns seen on grass or a windowpane on a winter's morning. A frost dragon is almost never seen in the daylight, yet with its pearlescent scales and horns made of diamond, it is one of the most exquisite of all dragons to behold.

Apprentice!

We have another clue to the whereabouts of the celestial dragon, sourced from our friend in the Beardmore Glacier.

CLIMB THE STEPS WHERE THE HEAVENLY NUMBER SITS THRICE SIDE BY SIDE.

Please make an appointment in my diary to assess all clues thus far. It is becoming clear that we will have to be in the right place at exactly the right time …

THE DRAGON PROTECTOR

SOUTH AMERICA

TERRAIN FOCUS

from one extreme to another

South America is one of the world's most biodiverse continents. This enormous variety of living things, both plant and animal, is good news for hungry dragons who want to eat a balanced diet.

These dragons make their homes in remarkable spots like the world's highest uninterrupted waterfall, Angel Falls in Venezuela, or the highest capital city, La Paz in Bolivia, or the world's largest rainforest, the Amazon Rainforest in Brazil. But the thing the dragons love most about South America . . . ? It is shaped like a dragon's claw!

Common Species of Dragon in South America

Welcome to the South America quarters of the *Dragon Ark*, where Chief Medic, Dr. Kolisi, is caring for a hydra who keeps passing the highly contagious dragon mouth disease between its many heads. No amount of cajoling will persuade a hydra to keep its heads apart.

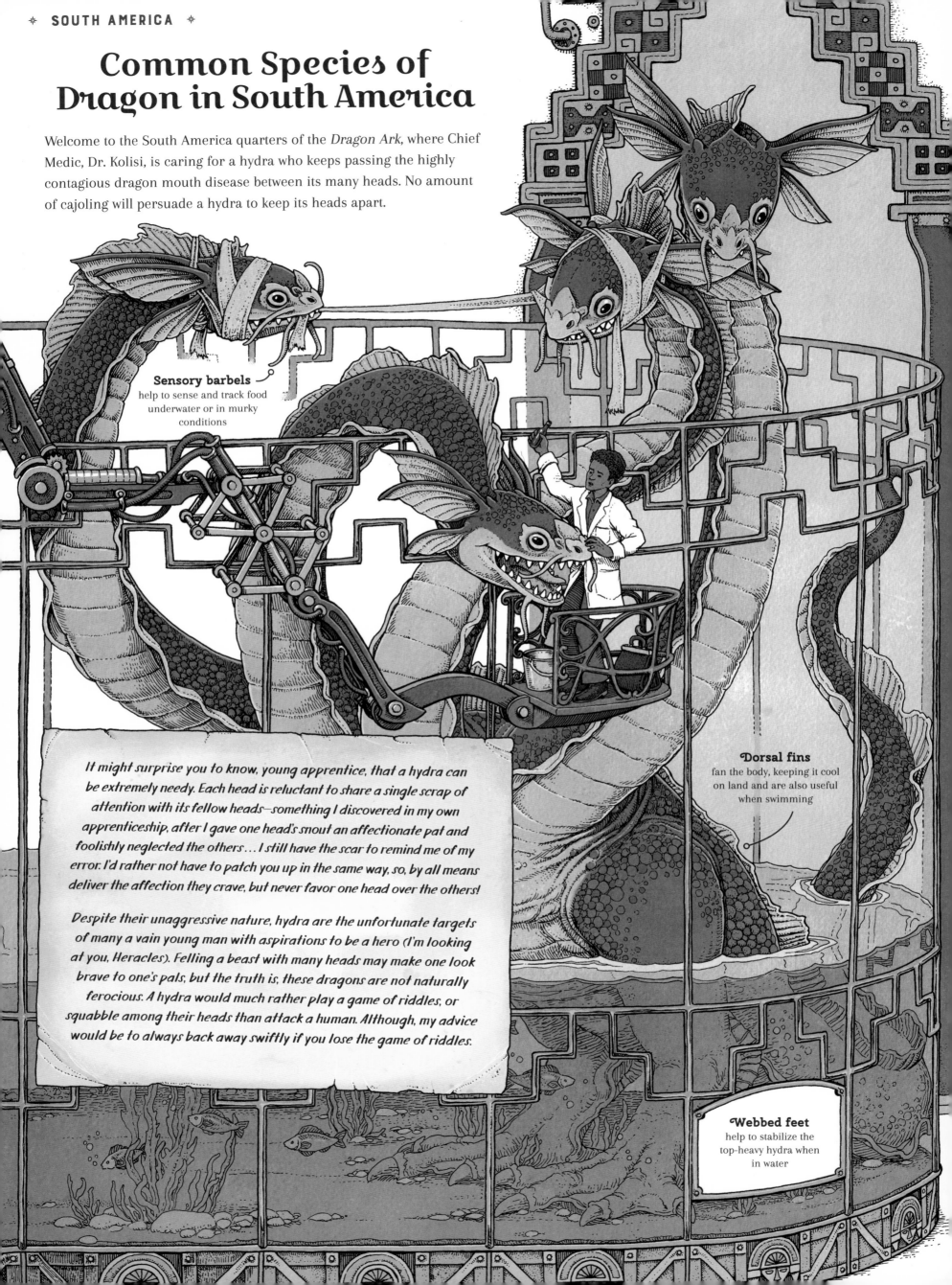

Sensory barbels
help to sense and track food underwater or in murky conditions

Dorsal fins
fan the body, keeping it cool on land and are also useful when swimming

It might surprise you to know, young apprentice, that a hydra can be extremely needy. Each head is reluctant to share a single scrap of attention with its fellow heads—something I discovered in my own apprenticeship, after I gave one head's snout an affectionate pat and foolishly neglected the others… I still have the scar to remind me of my error. I'd rather not have to patch you up in the same way, so, by all means deliver the affection they crave, but never favor one head over the others!

Despite their unaggressive nature, hydra are the unfortunate targets of many a vain young man with aspirations to be a hero (I'm looking at you, Heracles). Felling a beast with many heads may make one look brave to one's pals, but the truth is, these dragons are not naturally ferocious. A hydra would much rather play a game of riddles, or squabble among their heads than attack a human. Although, my advice would be to always back away swiftly if you lose the game of riddles.

Webbed feet
help to stabilize the top-heavy hydra when in water

The stories told among South American dragons never cease to surprise and amaze me. We should always seek to look beyond what we think we know when it comes to dragonkind…

The Llullaillaco Volcano

The seven-headed fire-breathing dragon Ihuaivulu once inhabited the Llullaillaco Volcano on the Argentina-Chile border. When the reclusive, peace-loving hydra discovered that three Inca children, whose mummifed bodies were recently discovered, had been unnecessarily sacrificed to appease it, Ihuaivulu was distraught and sought refuge on the *Dragon Ark* to prevent such a sacrifice from happening again. Today, Llullaillaco lies dormant, now that its fire-breathing resident has gone.

The Hydra: a Brief Study

Hydra are well-known for their abundance of heads. The amount and properties of each head entirely depends on the dragon's parentage. When a three-headed hydra mates with another three-headed hydra, a six-headed hatchling is almost guaranteed. The Dragon Protector came across one hydra with sixteen heads. She kept a very respectable distance.

The most powerful hydra are those with heads that display individual defenses. The hydra currently on board the ark can simultaneously breathe fire, ice, and poisonous gas, and spit venom, should it be provoked. For this reason, it is always best to avoid angering a hydra, unless you have your wits about you.

Stories have circulated since ancient times about the regenerative abilities of a hydra, and in particular, its ability to grow back a head once cut off. Dragon Protectors through the ages have decreed that this is nothing more than a cruel myth, yet many hydra have suffered unnecessarily because humans have wanted to test the theory for themselves. All that humans will discover is certain death in the jaws of the remaining heads!

The Pororoca

Around the time of the lunar equinox, a natural phenomenon called the Pororoca occurs, sending 13-foot-high waves up the Amazon River, against the current. Human surfers come from far and wide to ride these special waves, but little do they know that sea serpent dragons do, too. It's an excellent method of transportation for sea serpents wishing to visit family members living many miles away along the Amazon.

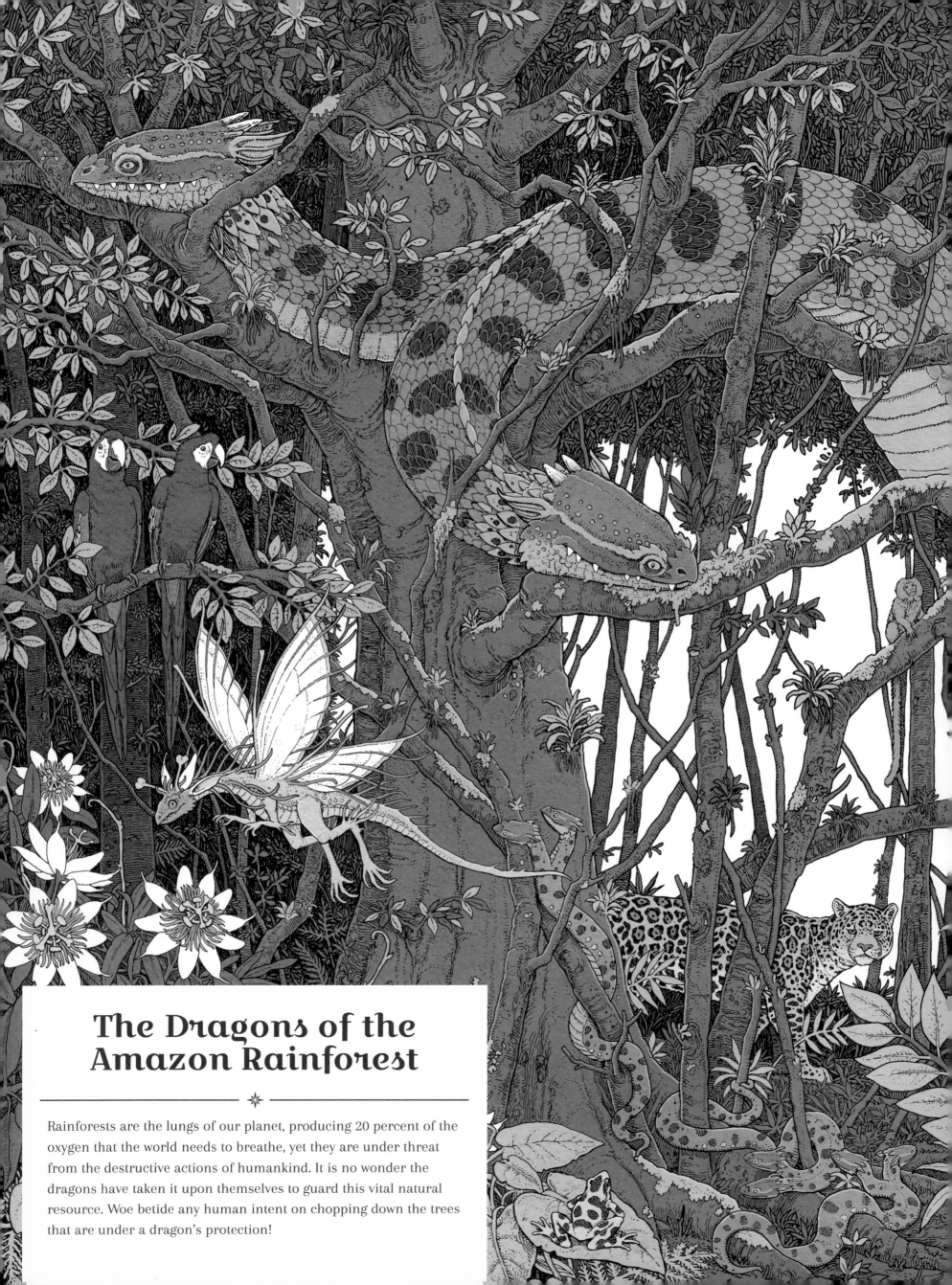

The Dragons of the Amazon Rainforest

Rainforests are the lungs of our planet, producing 20 percent of the oxygen that the world needs to breathe, yet they are under threat from the destructive actions of humankind. It is no wonder the dragons have taken it upon themselves to guard this vital natural resource. Woe betide any human intent on chopping down the trees that are under a dragon's protection!

Guardians of the Rainforest

The Dragon Protector has made a remarkable discovery while visiting the guardian dragons of the rainforest—an entirely new species of miniature dragons! You are most fortunate to have been present at this exciting moment in dragon natural history.

It is not every Dragon Protector who has the honor of discovering a new species of dragon. Incredible as it may be, it is yet unsurprising that the discovery should happen in the Amazon Rainforest, a place well-known for its immense biodiversity, and indeed one that non-dragon scientists agree is likely to contain many undiscovered species. I'll wager they weren't including dragons in that summary!

I have invited these creatures, which I have named parvula dragons—after parva, Latin, meaning "small"—to come aboard the ark for further study and introduction to our team. Some have graciously accepted, and I cannot wait to share our findings.

Much of the credit for this new discovery must go to the hydra that we had come to the rainforest to observe. An old friend of the Dragon Protectors and ally in the preservation of the rainforest and the dragons that live within it, we were hard-pressed to track it down on this occasion. Dwelling in the high canopy as it does, where the foliage is thick and the opportunities for camouflage great, it is already hard to spot with the naked eye, however this hydra had relocated further in for safety, amid rumors of deforestation. And it was there that we encountered our new dragon friends.

I am pleased that this rumor of imminent deforestation was just that— nothing more than rumor, likely circulated by a particularly malicious parrot, but I feel the Dragon Ark must return to this site sooner rather than later to ensure the continuing safety of the rainforest dragons.

Passifloracea

Parvula dragons

Early studies have revealed the newly discovered parvula dragons to be a truly diminutive species, even when fully grown. With a wingspan of between 4 and 6 inches, these dragons display qualities more regularly observed in butterflies, such as transparent wings covered by thousands of tiny, light-reflecting scales.

They also have a pair of antennae—useful appendages indeed for dragons living on the forest floor, where only a minimal amount of the sun's light can reach. Antennae help the dragons smell, but also to navigate their surroundings.

They eat a diet of grubs and insects, but are also partial to nectar and other sweet treats, like butterflies are. Each parvula has a chosen flower, and it seems that each dragon has evolved to resemble its favorite bloom in color and patterning. Perhaps for camouflage, although further studies will be required to confirm this.

Note: It may be important to maintain secrecy around the discovery of this new species, given their desirability as small, colourful, attractive pets. Should non-dragon-protecting humans discover the parvula, these dragons may be caught and imprisoned in cages against their will. It is recommended that the *Dragon Ark* increase its observation of the Amazon Rainforest forthwith.

B

Dear apprentice,

You are needed on the North America quarters. Please add the following clue to our notes on the whereabouts of the celestial dragon, obtained from the rainforest hydra:

THE AUSPICIOUS DAY IS ONLY UNLUCKY FOR SOME.

Let us hope the malicious parrot was not its source...

THE DRAGON PROTECTOR

NORTH AMERICA

TERRAIN FOCUS
presidents and pinnacles

Dragons in North America have had to be exceptionally cunning in order to remain undetected. Cover can be hard to come by on the wide-open prairies of Alberta or Montana or in the busy metropolises of New York or Mexico City.

Luckily, this is a continent that is also blessed with a wealth of ideal dragon nesting spots, found in its many mountain ranges or within natural wonders such as the breathtaking Grand Canyon, which many visitors may not realize is home to many shy dragon families.

Common Species of Dragon in North America

Tread lightly and breathe softly while on the North America quarters. A drake is in residence, and these dragons are extremely reclusive. Even an ill-timed sneeze could send it back into the depths of its stable, and the Dragon Protector would have to work through the night to coax it out.

Teeth
are constantly growing, with a newer, sharper set ready to replace the old

Missing scale
is the only chink in this seemingly invulnerable beast's armor

Working with drakes will take the patience of an owl and the courage of a lion, but never give up on them! You'll know when they trust you, for they'll display the spot on their stomachs where they're missing a scale. This is the only place these dragons can be pierced with a weapon and killed, so they are displaying their vulnerability to you. Protect that trust at all costs!

As with its cousin, the wurm, a drake's body parts are said to have certain properties that humans have tried to exploit for their own gain. The worst offenders are those who believe that bathing in a drake's blood will make their skin as hard as iron. That is, of course, ridiculous, and I will happily shut anyone who tries it in their own cave for a very long time.

Gowrows in the Ozarks

In 1897, one William Miller killed a gowrow, a huge beast described locally in Arkansas as a "wingless dragon with tusks." Miller swore he'd shipped the dragon's body to the Smithsonian Institution in Washington D.C., but the Smithsonian has always denied receiving it. Few people know that the incumbent Dragon Protector stepped in to retrieve the body before it was put on display, thus keeping the presence of dragons in the United States a secret.

As the Dragon Ark's librarian likes to remind us—history books will only tell one side of a dragon's story. Here's a cautionary tale or two of how the timely intervention of Dragon Protectors has protected dragons in the United States.

THE GREEN GOWROW, KILLED IN SEARCY COUNTY.

The Drake: a Brief Study

Drakes are intensely fearsome creatures. They have no wings and no other capability for flight—magical or otherwise. But what they lack in airborne power, they more than make up for in brute strength.

Drakes were often used as weapons in the battles recorded in ancient lore, for they have armored scales that are impenetrable to human sword or spear. There is always one missing scale, the only vulnerability in a drake's body, but no attacker will ever get close enough to discover where that scale is located.

These dragons can grow up to 40 feet in length. This enormous size, combined with their desire to live a solitary life, often sees them making their nests in caves and other secluded places. This drake came on board the ark when its home became the chosen location of some extreme sports fanatics' spelunking trip.

Dragons in the subway

New York City's disused Atlantic Avenue Tunnel—the world's oldest subway tunnel, according to Guinness World Records—was built in 1844. The public could tour the tunnel until the Department of Transportation closed it. People said it was because of safety concerns but in reality, it was the arrival of a family of drakes seeking a new home. The Dragon Protector made use of her governmental contacts to see to it that the dragons would remain safe beneath the city.

Drakes in the Rockies

Mountains offer the reclusive drake a perfect hiding place, and none more so than the colossal Rocky Mountains, stretching for some 3,000 miles from Canada to New Mexico. However, dragons of all types are also drawn to the Rockies for the minerals hidden within the mountains, particularly in the range that passes through Colorado—a state rich in many different minerals.

Top secret

AN ACCOUNT OF THE MOUNT RUSHMORE DRAGONS, 1939

by Rokeby Norris Esq.,
Dragon Protector

As is often the case, a chance meeting led me to the discovery of dragonkind in a land that is not mine. Minding my own business in a hostelry in the charming town of Keystone, South Dakota, a fellow covered in fine granite dust made my acquaintance—a driller, freshly returned from carving the gargantuan face of President Theodore Roosevelt on nearby Mount Rushmore. After several jars of the excellent local brew, he proceeded to recount the tall tale of a creature he swore he saw appear in the eye of Roosevelt as he drilled. "Teeth like needles," he said. "Eyes like demons."

In disguise as a humble traveler in these United States of America, I kept my own counsel. But as Dragon Protector, I knew without a doubt that this was proof of dragons living in the Black Hills. That was a remarkable discovery on its own, but I was yet to make the biggest discovery of all.

Enlisting the mountaineers among my crew back on the *Dragon Ark*, we scaled Mount Rushmore in the dead of night and ascended to the eye of Roosevelt. Lo, the dragon revealed itself—an amphiptere hatchling! After some reassurance, it guided us to the opening of its cave, deep inside the mountain, behind the presidents' mighty granite heads.

There—I can barely summon the words to do the sight justice—was revealed a hoard of treasure filling the cavern as far as the eye could see. Gold upon gold, glittering gemstones of every color of the rainbow, and diamonds the size of my head, scattered like dewdrops at the dawn of a spring morning.

And, more remarkably, guarding the hoard was an adult amphiptere, the beauty of which I have not seen outside of the famed amphipteres of Mexico. As befits an amphiptere, it had two feathered wings and no limbs, but this dragon had the most dazzling rainbow scales. My hypothesis remains that over decades inside the cavern, this dragon had absorbed the properties of the minerals surrounding it. After informing the creature that there was refuge to be found aboard the *Dragon Ark*, should the work on Mount Rushmore put it under threat, I bade it farewell with the Dragon Protector's solemn oath of utmost secrecy.

As I write, I am painfully aware of the dangers these dragons will face if discovered by treasure seekers or bounty hunters. But still, it must be scribed for the benefit of the Dragon Protectors that follow me. This account should therefore only be seen by those most trustworthy members of a Dragon Protector's crew, for even good men can be turned by greed.

*Rokeby
Norris Esq.*

Mountain Dragons

❖

The Dragon Protector has returned from her North American expedition with many exciting observations and fresh dragonate knowledge. Be sure to pay close attention—you may be visiting the same locations to check on the same dragons in the years to come.

Checking on dragons mentioned in the accounts of previous Dragon Protectors is a vital part of the job of a Dragon Protector. These creatures that one visits on a regular basis can become trusted advisors and friends, although I would counsel you to avoid attempting friendship with the rather grumpy drake in the Guilá Naquitz cave northwest of the Mitla site in Mexico. That dragon will stab you with a claw on a good day and BURN YOU TO A CRISP on a bad one …

But I digress. The Mount Rushmore amphiptere discovered by my predecessor, Rokeby Norris, is alive and well. The hatchling has since flown the nest, going south to live with its Mexican cousins, but it returns on its mother's birthday and the summer solstice.

It seems that the treasure is still intact, although it remains that discovery of the hoard and its guardian is never more than one coincidence away. The amphiptere regaled me with the tale of the movie crew scouting for a location for their latest cinematic endeavor, who missed the entrance to its cave by a whisker (or rather, the width of Abraham Lincoln's right nostril).

Dear apprentice, I do hope that at some point in your life you will visit this site. I have been blessed to see many wonders on my travels aboard the Dragon Ark, and the treasures that abound in this hidden corner of North America are enough to render one speechless. Just don't be tempted to remove any of them, for the amphiptere will see to it that you'll not see any more wonders—or anything else for that matter!

THE DRAGON PROTECTOR

MINERAL	Pyrite
PROPERTY	Flame igniter
FUNCTION	Encourages fire-breathing skills in dragon hatchlings

Drakes

We have known for some time that dragons like to absorb the properties of minerals, whether by ingesting them, rubbing their scales against them, or just basking in their energy. Our finest scientists are hard at work on board the ark to investigate whether minerals can be exploited for the further good of dragonkind—particularly in the field of dragon medicine. I am grateful to the family of mountain drakes I visited in Colorado, who have been most forthcoming on current trends in dragon mineral preferences, with one of their hatchlings particularly keen on pyrite.

MINERAL	Diamond
PROPERTY	Hardest natural substance on earth
FUNCTION	Popular among drakes for creating battle-ready scales

MINERAL	Aquamarine
PROPERTY	Rich color
FUNCTION	For the showy dragon, gives glorious blue color to scales

MINERAL	Barite
PROPERTY	Phosphorescent light
FUNCTION	Emits a green glow—useful for dragons living in caves

To be filed in celestial dragon clues:

LOOK TO THE CONSTELLATION THAT SEPARATES THE TWO BEARS

(Note: Clue was divulged by drake on North America quarters . . . Have seen its missing scale but still—is it a reliable source?)

EUROPE

into the woods

Many a dragon legend has taken root in the ancient woods and forests of Europe—and some of the dragons of those legends still live in peace here.

Dragons have felt completely at home in the hidden dells and secret caves of European forests, places that echo with an almost imperceptible magic, sheltered and protected by trees that have been there for hundreds of years. The trees and the dragons are entirely different beings, yet it seems there is an innate understanding and synergy between them.

Common Species of Dragon in Europe

Welcome to the Europe quarters, where you may feel a touch of magic in the air. The dragons aboard are wyverns, and they bring with them an age of mystical wisdom and legend. There are no better storytellers than wyverns, so spare some time to listen, should the opportunity arise.

Hypnotic voice can be used to immobilize an unfortunate listener

The wyvern certainly knows how to tell a tale, and while some are true, others are tall to say the least. I once found myself shimmying up the side of Big Ben in London, after believing a mischievous wyvern's story of a baby drake that had gotten itself wedged between three and four on the clockface.

With only two hind legs, and wings in place of front legs, these learned dragons would do anything to be able to hold and read a book for themselves. Should you wish to gain the eternal devotion of a wyvern, promise to read to it. It will gladly listen to anything you offer, be it a three-volume literary classic or your shopping list.

Tail aids in precision and maneuverability in the air

Our resident wyvern is something of an expert in the dragon lore of ancient Greece. His great-great-great-great-grandfather heard these stories firsthand and they have been passed down the generations. One thing's for sure— the ancient Greeks liked to use dragons to guard golden things...

The Golden Apples

Ladon, a hydra simply doing his job guarding the goddess Hera's precious golden apples, was killed by that irksome (and deeply unpopular among dragonkind) "hero," Heracles. One of these apples indirectly started the Trojan War, but our wyvern tells us that the golden apples from the story were, in fact, humble oranges. An awful lot of fuss for some citrus fruit!

The Wyvern: a Brief Study

Immortal celestial dragons aside, the wyvern is the dragon with the capability to live longest of all mortal dragons. This means that wyverns have patiently watched as history unfolds before them, drawing on this knowledge and becoming exceedingly wise.

Unfairly branded as vicious fire-breathers and maiden-eaters in medieval times, wyverns are largely peaceful, acting only to defend their young or the trees they protect. Fire-breathing is not conducive to a home surrounded by wood, so this will always be a last resort.

When the mood takes them, storytelling is the wyvern's true pastime of choice, and they have the power—rarely used maliciously—to hypnotize with their words. Of people reported missing in woods and forests each year, at least one or two can be explained by an encounter with a wyvern—not as a result of being eaten, but by being so captivated by a wyvern's story that they have lost all concept of time or space, often for weeks at a time.

The Golden Fleece

The Colchian dragon was chosen to guard Zeus's prize golden fleece because it could, reportedly, survive without sleep. Another "hero," Jason, was out to steal the fleece, and legend has it that some herbs he gave to the dragon put it to sleep. This couldn't have been further from the truth—all guardian dragons take their work very seriously—the dragon wasn't actually able to survive without sleep and was simply in dire need of a nap.

The Wyverns of Puzzlewood

The ancient woodland known as Puzzlewood in the United Kingdom has everything a wyvern longs for. With evidence of prehistoric settlement, Puzzlewood is home to many ancient and magical trees and has a ready supply of deer, rocks rich in iron ore, and, most importantly for a dragon who wishes to observe the comings and goings in the forest yet remain unseen, a natural underground system of hidden passageways known as scowles.

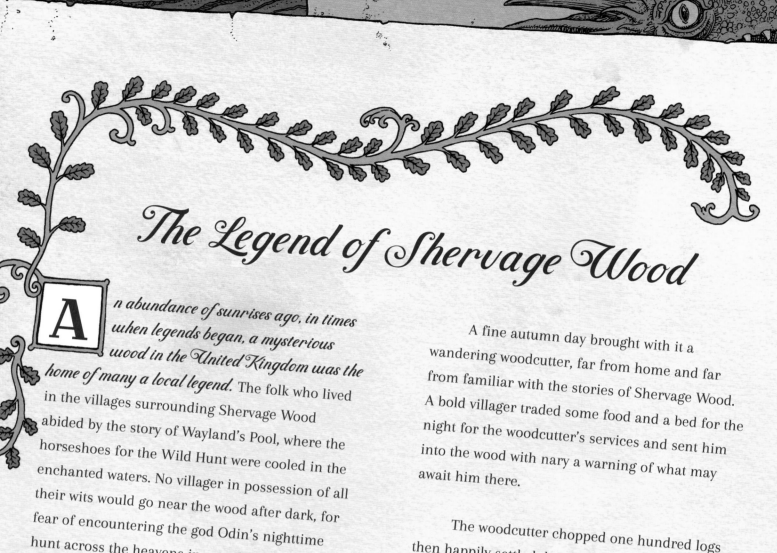

The Legend of Shervage Wood

An abundance of sunrises ago, in times when legends began, a mysterious wood in the United Kingdom was the home of many a local legend. The folk who lived in the villages surrounding Shervage Wood abided by the story of Wayland's Pool, where the horseshoes for the Wild Hunt were cooled in the enchanted waters. No villager in possession of all their wits would go near the wood after dark, for fear of encountering the god Odin's nighttime hunt across the heavens in search of the souls of the dead.

But now, they likewise feared to go in daylight. For a new enchantment had come upon the forest, in the form of the Shervage Wurm. It was a dragon, on whose shape and stature no one could speak for certain, but livestock and farm boys were vanishing aplenty and strange sounds were coming from the depths of the wood. The villagers were at their wits' end. The wood was a place of shelter, where they would pick berries, mushrooms, and healing herbs. Winter was coming and without logs from the wood for their hearths, the villagers would die from cold.

A fine autumn day brought with it a wandering woodcutter, far from home and far from familiar with the stories of Shervage Wood. A bold villager traded some food and a bed for the night for the woodcutter's services and sent him into the wood with nary a warning of what may await him there.

The woodcutter chopped one hundred logs then happily settled down on a fallen tree trunk to enjoy the villager's parcel of bread and cheese. But, no sooner had he taken one mouthful when the fallen tree trunk moved. The woodcutter spilled his provisions in surprise and jumped to his feet, axe in hand. When the trunk moved—this time before his very eyes—the woodcutter brought down his axe one, two, three times, splitting the tree trunk in half. But when one of the halves slunk away in one direction and the other half took the opposite path, the woodcutter dropped his axe in amazement. This was no tree.

The villagers showered the woodcutter in gifts of food and wine for saving them from the Shervage Wurm, and he never went hungry again.

2.30m

Athena—I would much appreciate you showing this to my apprentice, who needs to be aware of what happened in the dark days before the existence of the Dragon Protectors and the Dragon Ark.

That is, senseless killings of dragons who have the right to feed and take uninterrupted naps.

Many thanks,

THE DRAGON PROTECTOR

Forest-dwelling Dragons

The Dragon Protector always returns from visiting dragons in the forests of Europe with a fresh vigor and spring in her step. She encourages the entire crew to disembark from the ark, even for an hour, to breathe in the fresh, oxygenated air and let the trees' magic lift their spirits.

It's no wonder that many beloved books from modern literature are said to have been inspired by the enchanting Puzzlewood. (Note: Ask Athena for her reading list. The wyvern tells me one story involves a boy with a scar and another, some little chaps with hairy feet and a ring. Both sound excellent!)

On this expedition I was able to study Puzzlewood's scowles in greater detail, and note that they allow a dragon both a hiding place and a safe vantage point from which to observe all the comings and goings of humans. The history these dragons must have seen! After some cajoling, the wyvern we observed today confessed that he was the guardian of the hoard of 3,000 Roman-era coins found by Puzzlewood workers in one of the scowles in 1848. He still bears the shame of popping out for a snack, allowing the treasure be discovered.

There is much to be heartened by in the rest of this gloriously wooded continent, too, from the Black Forest in Germany to Tandövala ancient woodland in Sweden. We already knew that wyverns are forest-dwellers by choice, but this visit has allowed me to prove they will always make their home near to the oldest tree in a wood—in order to absorb some of that magic, but also to protect the tree from harm. The fiercest defenders of nature indeed.

A NEW CLUE FOR CONSIDERATION:

THE CELESTIAL DRAGON COMES ON THE SIXTH OF THE NIGHT'S BRIGHTEST LIGHT.

10

Leaves and Scales

When a dragon has lived awhile in the company of an ancient tree, its features start to mimic the shape of that tree's leaves. Studies continue on board the ark as to why this happens, but theories include both camouflage and magic. These are the observations the Dragon Protector was able to make on this European visit:

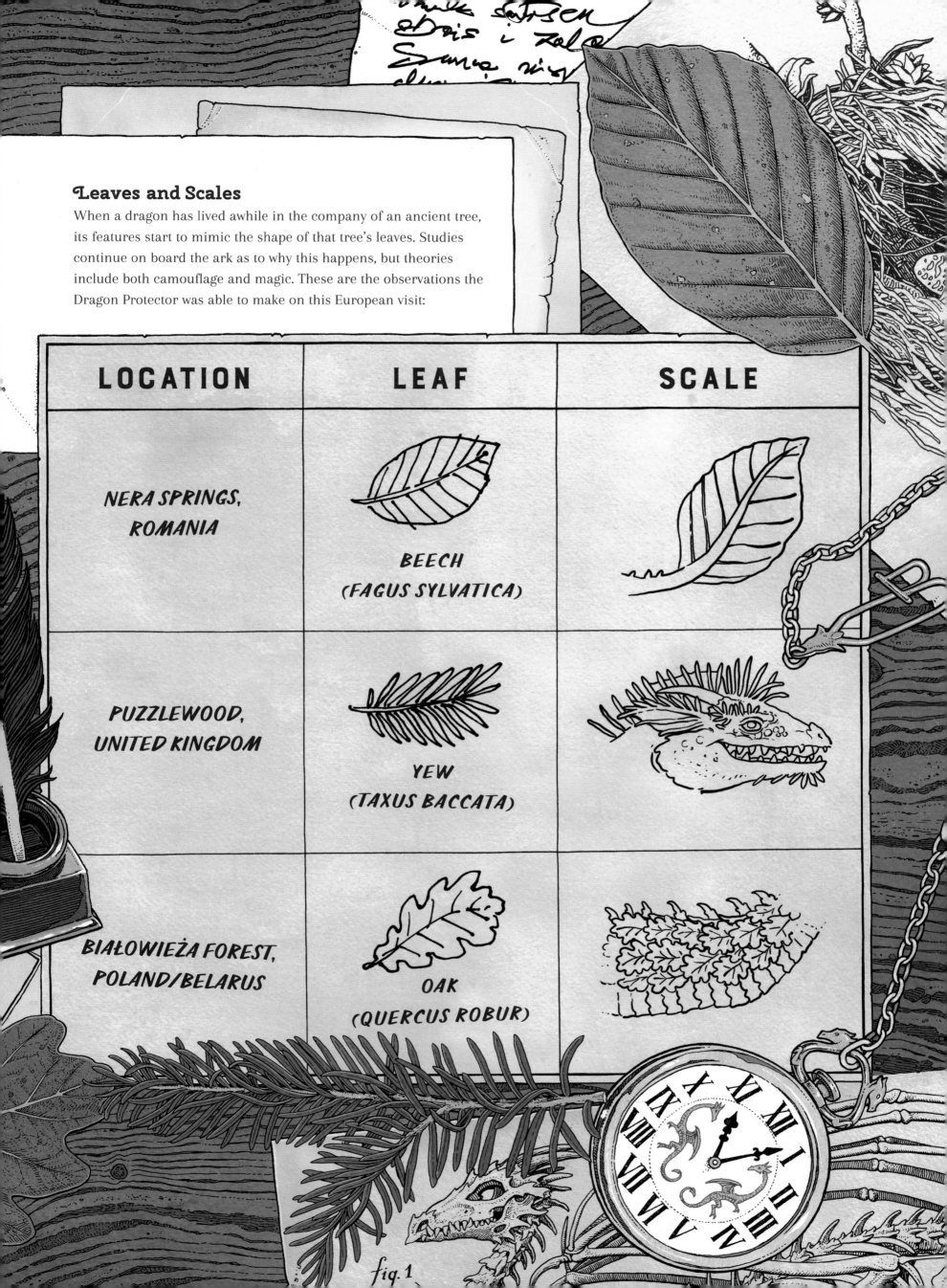

LOCATION	LEAF	SCALE
NERA SPRINGS, ROMANIA	BEECH (FAGUS SYLVATICA)	
PUZZLEWOOD, UNITED KINGDOM	YEW (TAXUS BACCATA)	
BIAŁOWIEŻA FOREST, POLAND/BELARUS	OAK (QUERCUS ROBUR)	

fig. 1

AFRICA

TERRAIN FOCUS

hot sands and cool waters

The fifty-four countries that make up this mighty continent enjoy terrain as diverse as the dragons that live here. With more than half of its surface made up of desert and drylands such as the famous Sahara, heat-loving dragons are in their element in this hot continent.

There is also plenty to delight the water-loving among dragonkind, with some of the world's most impressive waterfalls located in Africa. The Dragon Protector struggles to keep on top of the number of dragons living on the African continent as they thrive so heartily in their extreme surroundings. A nice problem to have, as she often says . . .

Common Species of Dragon in Africa

Come and bask in the warmth of the Africa quarters, where the Dragon Protector has stoked the furnaces in order to create a temperature akin to those found in the hottest continent on earth. The amphiptere has been furnished with everything to make it feel truly at home while on board, including its very own *Boswellia* tree.

Feathered wings
give a hint as to the amphiptere's evolutionary lineage

I could gaze upon this glorious dragon for days and days, my dear apprentice. You will no doubt be equally enticed, but a word of advice—NEVER WALK BENEATH IT! This dragon came to us from the Boswellia of northwest Ethiopia, and its innate drive to protect the trees' precious sap is not lowered just because it happens to be with us on the ark. It will stick you with its pointy tail without a moment's hesitation.

Now that I have shared news of its cousin in Mount Rushmore, this amphiptere has requested to stay aboard until we make another circle of the globe and return to North America, where it can visit in safety. The flight from Ethiopia to South Dakota is not one any right-minded dragon would wish to make alone, so of course I am happy to extend our hospitality. It will unfortunately mean extra dung-clearing duties for you, however. Such is the life of an apprentice!

Barbed tail
has a vicious spike that can be used to impale a victim

In Africa, as in all continents of the world, things considered to be natural phenomena are often the work of dragons. Of course, dragonkind are the most phenomenal of all, but I am biased ...

The Amphiptere: a Brief Study

The amphiptere has a long and distinguished past as a guardian, appearing in texts from antiquity such as Greek historian Herodotus's *The Histories*. With origins in North Africa and Mesoamerica, the modern African amphiptere has the same role as its ancestors: as protector of the precious sap of the *Boswellia* tree, which, when dried, is known as frankincense.

As guardians of these trees, amphiptere have a barbed tail that is used to protect the *Boswellia* from passing prey— or humans with malicious intent. When an unwelcome creature passes beneath the tree, the guardian amphiptere will make itself ramrod straight, tip backwards and plummet to the ground, tail first, to impale the poor unfortunate creature on its barb.

Their violent devotion toward their duty is belied by their dazzling physical form, with shimmering wings and enticingly enormous eyes, described by the ancient Egyptians as looking like peacock feathers. Used by their avian cousins to attract a mate, the amphiptere's eyes are simply ornamental, adding to the beauty of this extraordinary dragon.

Dragon's Breath Cave

One of Namibia's natural wonders, the cave contains an immense underground lake. It's too deep to explore, which allows the sea serpents who reside at the bottom to have an undisturbed life. The cave was named for the humid air that rose from its opening when discovered in 1986, but as dragon's breath is generally fetid enough to knock out a grown man, this is something of a romantic notion.

Saharan Sands

Even though the two locations are thousands of miles apart, an estimated 22,000 tons of phosphorus-rich dust from the Sahara in Chad ends up in the Amazon soil every year, nourishing its plants. Scientists have their theories as to how this occurs, but they really only need to look to the sand drakes, who have the power to stir up the dust and blow it to high enough altitudes for it to be caught by the winds and carried away.

Sand Dragons in the Sahara

✦

The enormity of the Sahara, which spans eleven different countries and covers 3.6 million square miles, is good news for the thriving dragon population living among its sand dunes, salt flats, and basins. These dragons have evolved to survive in the extreme conditions, and relish the privacy that the largest hot desert on earth provides.

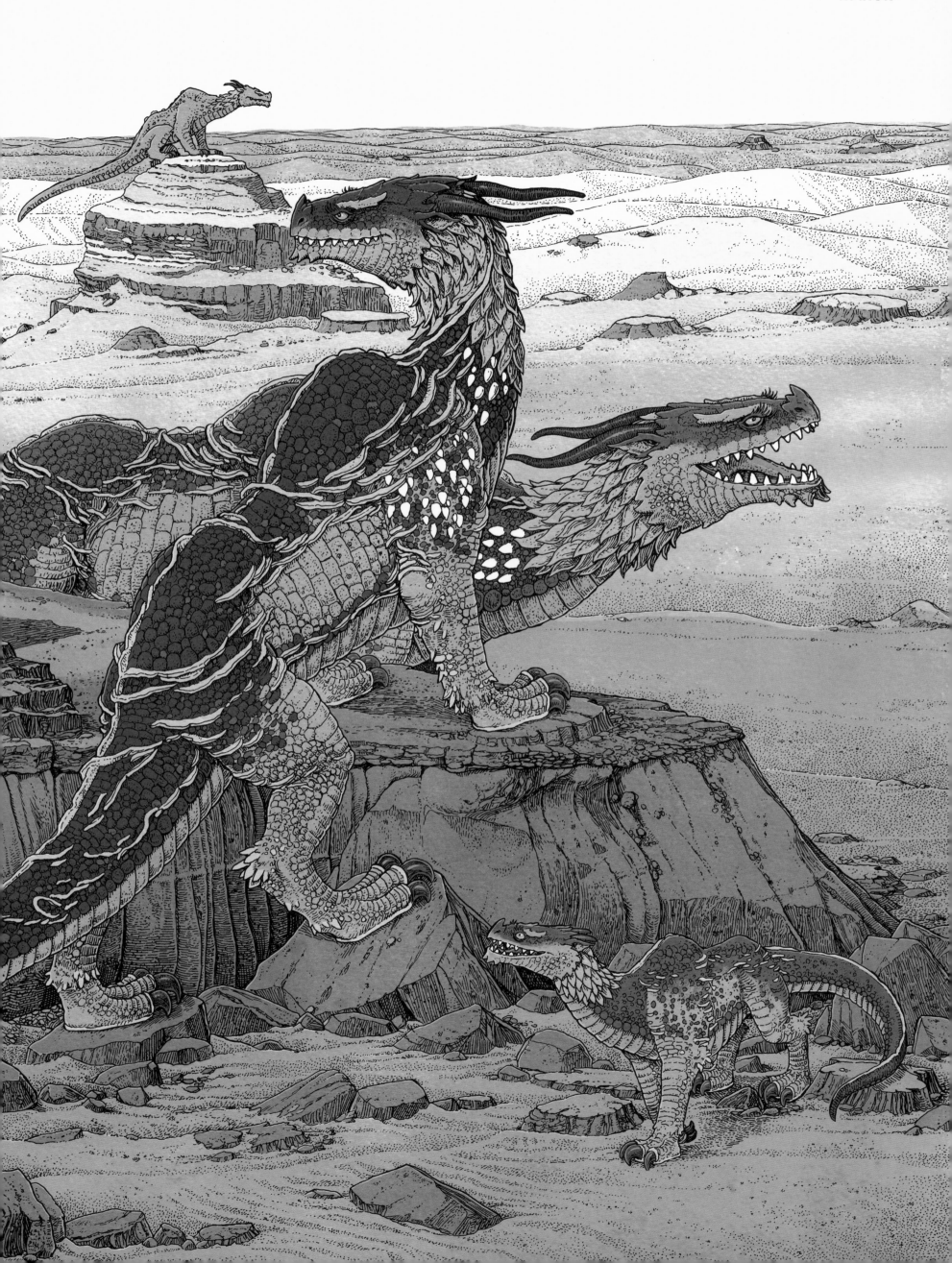

Dragons Behind the Waterfall

Fresh from the Mariana Trench, Dr. Chen has taken on another subaqueous mission on behalf of the Dragon Protector and the *Dragon Ark*. What's more, she has opened her notebook once again to share her findings with you.

Devil's Pool, Victoria Falls (Zambia side)

Thanks to a tip from our resident drake, I am thrilled to say that we have today discovered an entirely new family of water drakes living in a secret cave behind the spectacular Victoria Falls (or Mosi-oa-Tunya—the smoke that thunders—to use its local indigenous name). No other humans know of this cave's existence, bar those of us aboard the ark.

Who knew that beneath the shallow waters of the famous tourist attraction Devil's Pool lies the entrance to a hidden tunnel, which, if fortunate enough to know its precise location, one can slide down and end up in a huge cave directly behind the waterfall itself . . .

We did not stay long, for these dragons value their privacy, but long enough to discover that the drakes originally climbed 100 feet (vertically!) from the ground to reach the cave's opening. They survive on raptors and other large birds that unwittingly fly too close to the cave and are hidden from the eyes of tourists by the thunderous waters of the Zambezi River that crash over the ledge above.

Without wings, these drakes cannot leave their cave through flight, so the ark must make it a priority to visit them regularly and provide any supplies or medical care that they may need. I will be recommending to the Dragon Protector that we closely investigate other major waterfalls and search for dragonkind there. Iguazú Falls and Niagara Falls should be priorities.

The Sands of Dragon Time

This visit to the Sahara has helped the Dragon Protector gather fresh findings into how dragons have evolved to adapt to their surroundings. She has headed straight to her quarters to brief the ark's scientists—let's join her there.

BRIEFING: DRAGON PROTECTOR TO DR. KOLISI AND DR. SUN

Can report a thoroughly successful expedition to the Qattara Depression in Egypt; conditions were perfect for communing with sand drakes. My thanks, Dr. Sun, for providing a tank of water and food—the drakes were most amenable to talking once they had eaten and drunk their fill.

Some interesting new observations on sand drakes to be studied in greater detail:

1. The underside of each foot is padded with a layer of fat. This seems to make it easier and more comfortable for the dragons to walk on the hot sands. Do volcanic dragons have the same?

2. Several rounded humps are visible on the back— stores of fat that they can draw on for energy and hydration when food or water is scarce. Dr. Kolisi— can we bring equipment to Qattara to scan these humps?

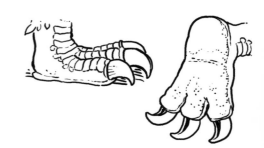

3. Unusually for dragons, the sand drakes have long, fine eyelashes, keeping the sand from their eyes.

4. The sand drakes prey on camels, but they seem to have more in common with their dromedary neighbors than they may choose to admit to!

This family were reluctant to come on board the ark, but are happy to receive Dr. Sun and her team for further tests to be carried out. Please see my apprentice to arrange.

D.P.

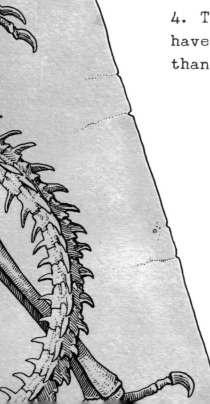

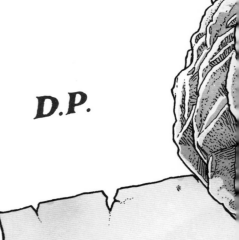

Pharaoh's pet

Not seen in the wild for many centuries, the ouroboros dragon—a dragon who bites its own tail, forming the shape of a circle—was first depicted on a golden shrine found in the tomb of the ancient Egyptian pharaoh Tutankhamun. Scholars have their own theories on the symbolism of the pharaoh's ouroboros, but the secret truth is that Tutankhamun was a fiercely loyal friend to dragons and kept an ouroboros as a beloved and overindulged pet.

Apprentice!

Please report to the Asia quarters immediately. With this clue, sourced by Dr. Chen from the water drakes of Victoria Falls, we are now ready to begin our search for the celestial dragon.

History will soon be made. I hope you are ready?

THE DRAGON PROTECTOR

ASCEND TO THE PLACE WHERE VAPOR MEETS DUST AND DROPLETS ARE FORMED.

ASIA

TERRAIN FOCUS
the dragon of legend

The final stop on the Dragon Ark's journey is Asia, the largest and most densely populated continent of them all.

Asia is extremely rich in natural resources—from the natural gas reserves of Russia to the minerals of China—of which the dragon population are immensely proud and immensely protective. The Dragon Protector will be making many lengthy excursions across the continent to visit all the dragons in her care, but the focus of the ark remains on one dragon in particular. For this is the home of the celestial dragon, which has so far evaded all Dragon Protectors. With extreme luck and a favorable following wind, this will be our best—and probably only—chance to see this incredible beast in its natural surroundings.

Common Species of Dragon in Asia

Greetings from the Asia quarters, where we are enjoying an environment of peace and tranquillity created by the loong dragon currently on board. The loong is the bringer of rain and maker of fertile lands, and is revered in Chinese mythology—and by everyone on the *Dragon Ark*. All crew members are invited to spend time in its benevolent presence, for their own well-being and sense of inner calm.

Take my word for it—you'll want to bring a comfy cushion with you when you visit the loong in its stable, as time simply flies by in its presence. I love to roll out my yoga mat in my cabin on a quiet evening, but spending even half an hour with this dragon will leave you feeling more peaceful than a lifetime of yoga ever could.

Different loongs have different responsibilities for specific areas of existence. This loong is a shenloong, the spiritual dragon that controls storms and the rain, so we have done our best to replicate cloud cover in its stable. You may want to avoid getting too close in case of an unexpected lightning strike.

There will be plenty of pearls of wisdom on offer to any humans who ask for them, alongside the real pearl the loong carries in its mouth. It is said that the powers of the loong's pearl will transfer to a human if the human gets hold of it, but don't go getting any ideas—not only is it not recommended to separate a loong and its precious gem, it would not be advisable for you to play with extreme weather …

Snout
is similar to a
crocodile's jaw

Fish scales
on its snakelike
body are like those
of the koi carp

Dragon stories have been part of Chinese culture for thousands of years, and while the symbol of a dragon is seen on many buildings, streets and we on the *Dragon Ark* know that there are real dragons living happy and fulfilled lives in China.

The Loong: a Brief Study

In this dragon's handsome features we see an echo of the ancient past. Each of the animals that represented the different tribes of ancient China can be recognized in the loong of today, namely—the scales of a koi carp, the antlers of a deer, a pig's nose, a snake's body, the claws of an eagle, a crocodile's jaws, and the eyes of a bull.

This loong has a magical pearl that it keeps safe inside its mouth. Other loong keep theirs embedded in their throat or forehead, according to their preference and physiology. The pearl gives the dragon its wisdom and power.

Unlike many of their Western cousins, loong do not have wings. This is thought to be because flying is powered by mystical forces and not by physical motion. The ark's chief aeronaut, Aurelius McGregor, and the rest of his flight team are always keen to question a loong when one is on board, to find out more about this extraordinary phenomenon. The gracious loong never fails to give them all the time and wisdom they seek.

Dragon or Drainage?

Bejing's Forbidden City, an impressive palace complex built between 1406 and 1420, has a revolutionary plumbing and drainage system worthy of modern times. With overflow waterspouts carved in the shape of dragon heads, it is very easy for a mischievous dragon to join the line-up of dragons in order to surprise unsuspecting tourists.

Dumplings and Dragon Boats

On the fifth day of the fifth month, the Dragon Boat Festival takes place throughout the country. Commemorating Qu Yuan, a beloved poet who drowned in the Miluo River more than 2,000 years ago, rice dumplings were thrown into the river to distract the fishes from the poet's body. Dumplings are now eaten on dry land instead of being thrown into the river, much to the dismay of the dumpling-loving dragons who live within its waters.

AL-KHAZNEH, PETRA, JORDAN

Al-Khazneh is the first structure a visitor will encounter when visiting the ancient city of Petra in Jordan. An extraordinary sight in the middle of the Arabian desert, Al-Khazneh means "the treasury" in Arabic, although no evidence of treasure has ever been found. Friends of dragons know the truth. Around 2,000 years old, this lofty cave, fronted by a majestic façade carved into the sandstone rock, is thought to have been a tomb for a king. A drake was stationed inside the tomb to protect the body of the king, who was also said to be a friend of dragonkind.

Over the years, the drake fulfilled its duty as guardian, guarding the tomb and scaring away any Bedouin tribesmen who ventured inside in search of the rumored treasure. But when this dragon died, there were no dragons available in the vicinity to take over as guardian. We can't pinpoint exactly when the looting happened, but visitors to Al Khazneh today will find the tomb entirely empty.

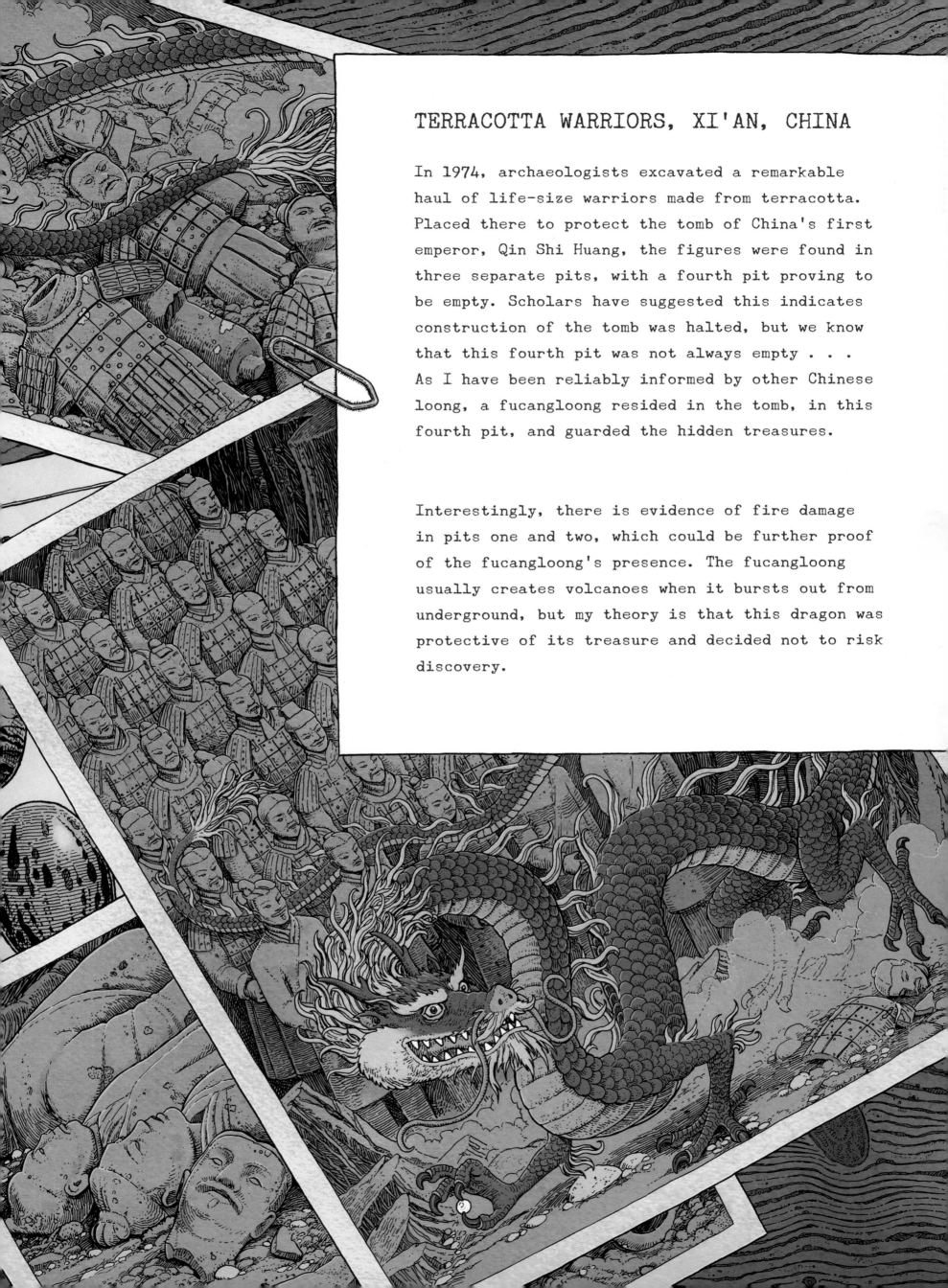

TERRACOTTA WARRIORS, XI'AN, CHINA

In 1974, archaeologists excavated a remarkable
haul of life-size warriors made from terracotta.
Placed there to protect the tomb of China's first
emperor, Qin Shi Huang, the figures were found in
three separate pits, with a fourth pit proving to
be empty. Scholars have suggested this indicates
construction of the tomb was halted, but we know
that this fourth pit was not always empty . . .
As I have been reliably informed by other Chinese
loong, a fucangloong resided in the tomb, in this
fourth pit, and guarded the hidden treasures.

Interestingly, there is evidence of fire damage
in pits one and two, which could be further proof
of the fucangloong's presence. The fucangloong
usually creates volcanoes when it bursts out from
underground, but my theory is that this dragon was
protective of its treasure and decided not to risk
discovery.

The Yangtze Dragons

※

This mighty river, the longest in Asia and the third longest in the world, flows for 3,915 miles. A favorite spot for loong is the first bend, which sees the river make an extraordinary switch from south to north, forming a V-shaped turn. Not only is there lush greenery on the riverbanks to hide in, the way the river flows mimics the bodies of the snakelike loong—a perhaps insignificant fact, but it pleases them greatly.

CLUE: The celestial dragon may only be found in the fifth zodiac year.

The year of the dragon.

CLUE: The auspicious day is only unlucky for some.

The thirteenth day.

CLUE: Look to the constellation that separates the two bears.

Draco.

CLUE: Climb the steps where the heavenly number sits thrice side by side.

There are 999 steps to the top of Tianmen Mountain.

CLUE: The celestial dragon comes on the sixth of the night's brightest light.

The sixth moon of the solar year (June).

CLUE: Ascend to the place where vapor meets dust and droplets are formed.

The clouds!

10 P.M.

We have followed all clues to our location, but it seems we are too late. The joy of finding a nest was soon met by the sorrow of finding it empty. I cannot understand what I have missed... The clouds that surround us are now matching my gloomy mood.

10.45 P.M.

The cloud cover is becoming worse. Aurelius has advised that flying the craft will be dangerous if we stay here much longer, but I simply cannot return to the ark with the news that we have failed to find the celestial dragon. I *cannot*.

11.59 P.M.

It is impossible to believe what my eyes are seeing! The clouds have finally parted, and—well, for the first time in my life, I am utterly and entirely speechless...

THE CELESTIAL EGG

Unlike the egg of a Western dragon, a celestial dragon's egg resembles a large crystal and gives off moisture whenever there is rain. A dragon hatchling is said to have incubated for 3,000 years before it hatches, but I am yet to gain confirmation of this fact from the adult dragons. The hatchling will grow to its juvenile size extremely fast. I'd try not to be in its way when this happens.

MY DEAR APPRENTICE!

Today, we have succeeded where many before us have failed. We have located the celestial dragon, guardian of the heavens and the dragon that Dragon Protectors have sought for generations. And—wonder of wonders—there is a hatchling! I dreamed of this glorious moment of discovery for decades, but what we have found here goes beyond all my hopes. The risk of extinction is, at least, lessened.

The celestial dragon pair have decided to come aboard the ark with their hatchling, where Dr. Sun and Dr. Kolisi shall observe them. Precious cargo indeed! We must guard them with our lives.

To another matter... As you may have realized, I am not much given to praise, but you have proved yourself on this voyage, and I would be delighted to appoint you as a Dragon Protector-in-waiting. Your first responsibility will be to care for the celestial hatchling, while I study its parents. We must always strive to protect these magnificent creatures, and I know you will be a worthy successor when the time comes. Note: Some dung clearing will still be required.

Now, let's hurry to the lab and settle in the newest residents of the *Dragon Ark!*

YOURS IN FIRE AND ICE,

CURATORIA DRACONIS

THE DRAGON PROTECTOR